Contents

Chapter 1
Well Done Me

HAH! Well done me!

I am The Wickedest Witch in the World!.

Yes, it's official.

I've just won the 'Wickedest Witch' Contest!

I got big silver cup with my name on the side.

Old Maggit
The Wickedest Witch in the World

That's what it said. I also got a black balloon, a baddy bag and a year's free supply of mint caterpillars from Yuckies, the sweet makers. Mind you, I've given Yuckies plenty of custom in the past. It takes a LOT of sweets to cover a whole house.

The other witches were a bit miffed. The Sea Witch turned green with envy – well, greener. Baba Yaga stormed out in a huff and wouldn't even stay for the party. She reckons she's famous back in Russia, or wherever she comes from. I say she's a bad loser, like the rest of them.

They all stood around giving me the evil eye and grumbling about the lack of comfy seats. We witches tend to be old. Chairs mean a lot to us. But not as much as giving little kiddies nightmares and winning contests.

The 13th Fairy took it worse than the others. She's called Grimbleshanks. She scuttled up to me at the supper table, where I was heaping my plate with yummy crispy spiders. The food is always good at these events. They know what witches like. As well as the plate, I was holding my winner's cup, a glass of fizzy wine, the black balloon and the baddy bag, so I had my hands full. It wasn't a good time, but I was up to it.

"Hello, Grimbleshanks," I said. "Well done on coming last."

"Shut up, Maggit," she said. "This is so unfair. You can't even spin. You never ride your broomstick. And I bet you've never ever put a whole palace of people to sleep for a hundred years."

"Hang on," I said. "I push little children into ovens. That's a lot more wicked than a daft little sleep spell."

She said, "Well, I think it's a scandal. I would like to remind you that you got pushed into the oven yourself in the end. By rights, you shouldn't even be here."

I said, "Ah, but I used a spell to put the fire out, didn't I? That took quick thinking. And look who's talking! This is the Wickedest *Witch* contest. You're not a witch, you're a fairy."

"A *bad* fairy," she snapped. "That's the same as a witch."

"Tell that to the judges," I said, with a sneer. "I won and you lost. Get over it." And I strolled off to have my picture taken.

The party didn't last long. Witches don't get on with each other at the best of times, never mind when they have just lost a contest. They all stayed just long enough to eat all the food, then the fighting began. There were the usual thunderbolts and flashes of green lightning and shouted curses. A number of people got turned into frogs and someone set fire to the curtains. It was quite a free-for-all.

I didn't join in. I had nothing to prove. I just stood there with a smug smile, drinking the fizzy wine and hugging my cup.

At last, everyone went home and I got the chance to inspect my baddy bag. There was a fake rubber worm, some cheap sparklers and a set of plastic fingernails. All around me, the staff were stacking up chairs, sweeping the filthy floor and chasing out the frogs. They made it very clear that I was in their way.

So I went home. I fed my cat, Wilson, and made myself a cup of tea. I set the silver cup in pride of place over the fire and sat down to look at it.

The Wickedest Witch in the World.

That was me.

It was a dream come true.

Chapter 2
My Brilliant Idea

I suppose I should tell you how it came about. You'll have heard the story, of course. About the poor wood-cutter who took a new wife and let his dopey kids wander off into the forest. Hansel and Gretel, they're called. You're supposed to feel sorry for them, what with their rubbish parents and the way they get lost and have me to deal with and all. But there are two sides to every story.

I had been dying to win the Wickedest Witch title for years, but I'd never even got on the short-list. The contest is held every year and is always judged by the same three big cheeses. That's the White Witch from Narnia, the Snow Queen from somewhere up north and the Wicked Witch of the West. Her dressing room is full of crates of bananas because she always brings her troupe of flying monkeys. She's a bit of a diva, by all accounts.

Anyway.

Year after year, I filled out the form and sent it in. I had to write up to ten sentences to say why I felt I should be in the contest. Here's what I wrote –

My name is Old Maggit. I live in a house in the forest. I have a pointy hat and a cat called Wilson. I cackle over my cauldron (extra-loud at full moon). My favourite food is crispy spiders. My favourite colour is black. I am dead scary.

Every year, the contest people wrote back to tell me I had not been selected. They said that what I wrote could apply to pretty much any witch. There were some very wicked witches out there, they said, and I would need to do something much more dramatic if I wanted to stand a chance.

It had begun to get to me.

It was clear I needed to come up with something a bit different. Something that would make me stand out. Something so dark, so daring, so dreadful that it would pass into folklore as well as win me the cup. I thought about it all the time. I filled up a whole notepad with ideas, but they had all been done before or they weren't bad enough.

And then it came to me! An idea so brilliant that I couldn't believe nobody had thought of it.

I would make a gingerbread house and decorate it with sweets. A beautiful little house in the deep, dark forest that no kiddy could pass by. It would be the perfect honey trap.

At that point, I'll admit I hadn't really worked the whole thing out properly. Once the kiddies were in my power, I wasn't sure what I would *do* with them. But I felt sure I would come up with something. Perhaps I could hold them to ransom. Make them clean the cooker. Lock them in the naughty shed. At the least I would give them a stern lecture about not going into strangers' houses. Anyway, I would think about that bit later. I was keen to get started.

It made sense to do up my own house, rather than build something new. After all, it only needed to be changed on the outside. That way, Wilson and I could carry on living there without any big changes. Wilson hates change. He likes his own cat flap, and his usual place by the fire.

I ordered the gingerbread panels for the walls and the sweet decorations from Yuckies. They were quite surprised and kept asking if I was sure I needed so much stuff. It wasn't often they got such a huge order. As you might expect, it cost me a fortune, but I was sure that it would be worth it in the long run.

I got in a firm of local builders to do the real work. It's always best to use experts. It can get very messy when you're building with treacle and marzipan. And barley sugar windows are trickier than you would believe.

The builders were called Frank, Ted and Rocky. They did a lot of noisy hammering and caused no end of mess. I was glad when they finished. I was tired of them dragging icing sugar into the house on their boots and demanding endless cups of tea.

The house took three days to complete. But, oh my! What a result! My humble cottage was gone. In its place stood a vision of chocolate

roof-tiles, candy chimneys, marzipan window sills, fudge shutters, lollipop flowers, and toffee doors. I was so pleased, I even gave the builders a tip.

I said, "Here's a tip. Wipe your feet before you come into people's houses. Goodbye."

Well, I'm a witch. What do you expect?

Chapter 3
The Kidnap

A sweet house has its downsides, to tell the truth. Small forest animals and insects tend to get stuck to it. I was always going round peeling off rabbits and small hedgehogs and picking off flies. The birds pecked off all the red Smarties, for some reason. But at least the sun didn't shine, so the roof didn't melt. I felt sure that it wouldn't be long before some kiddies came along. All I had to do was sit inside, keep an eye on the window, and wait.

On the third day, I was in my chair by the window watching the sun set when I heard voices. Young, high voices that rang through the forest. I ducked behind the curtain and crept across to the door. My first victims! How exciting!

I stooped down and peered through the letterbox. Two children had appeared out of the trees – a boy of about twelve, I thought, and a small girl who looked about six. I'm not good with children's ages. Or children, come to that. I prefer cats.

The boy wore a coat and leggings and a stupid hat with a feather. The girl wore a green cape. She trailed behind the boy, crying loud sobs. Oh dear. A weeper. That could get annoying.

"Come *on*, Gretel!" the boy shouted. He sounded really bossy. "Why are you always so *slow*!"

The girl lifted her little wet, red face and roared, "I'm *hungry*, I'm telling you! I don't want to walk any more!"

"Too bad. Keep up. You're such a baby."

"I *hate* you, Hansel. I'm telling *Daddy*!"

The boy was just about to answer back, when he spotted my house. His mouth fell open. The girl followed his gaze and her eyes opened wide. I moved away from the letterbox. I didn't want them to see me peering out. That might put them off.

"Sweets!" I heard the boy shout. "It's a house made of *sweets*!"

The girl gave a squeal of joy. There came the sound of running feet, and then they were at the door.

"Get back!" the boy shouted. "*I'm* having the marzipan!"

"Well, I'm having the lollipop flowers, then."

"No you're not! I'm having the red ones!"

"I'm telling *Daddy!*"

Now was my big moment. They were right outside. But I needed them *inside*. The moment they set foot inside the door, they would be in my power. That's the way it works. But they had to do it of their own free will. I would need as much charm as I could muster. I would normally throw the door open with a wild cackle, but today that would not do.

I snatched off my pointy hat and threw it in a corner. It hit my broomstick, which fell over and hit Wilson. He spat at me.

"Sssh," I hissed. "Be a good boy, Wilson, if you please."

I put my hand on the door knob and called out, in a gentle, shaky sort of voice.

"Who is that nibbling at my house? Little children, is it? I do hope so. I so *love* little children."

There was a moment's shocked hush. I put on my best welcoming smile. Then I opened the door.

The boy stood staring at me. He had a chunk of gingerbread in one hand and a bunch of red lollipop flowers in the other. The girl had broken off the door knob and was getting stuck in. Her cheeks were all shiny and sticky. Some sugar was in her hair.

"Who are you?" the boy demanded. Talk about rude. I had to fight the urge to snatch off his daft hat and throw it in a tree.

"I'm the kind old lady who lives here," I said. "You can call me Old Maggit. And who might you be, deary?"

"I'm Hansel," he said, "and that's my sister, Gretel. If you *must* know."

"And what are you doing here, so far from the path?" I asked. "Are you lost?"

"No," said Hansel. "I'm running away from home. *She* just tagged along after me."

"He's always doing that," said Gretel, as she broke off a piece of window-frame and stuffed it down her throat. "Running away, I mean."

"Any particular reason you run away so often?" I asked.

"I'm not happy with the food at home," said Hansel. He folded his arms and looked pompous. "I want to go to boarding school, where they have decent meals. But my step-mother says she and my father can't afford it. So I'm running away in protest. Can all of this house be eaten, or just the outside?"

"Why don't you step inside and see for yourself?" I offered. "I'll make you a lovely mug of hot milk and some fresh bread and butter."

"Not likely, "said Hansel. "We'll stick with the sweets."

"What about pancakes?" I said. "I'll let you toss them in the frying pan." That tempted them.

"*I* want to toss first," said Gretel, and made for the door.

"No," said Hansel. "*I* do. I'm the oldest." And he shoved her aside and pushed past me.

Gretel let out a scream and said, "I *hate* you, Hansel. I'm telling *Daddy*."

They really were most unpleasant children.

Chapter 4
Into the Naughty Shed

Once they were inside, things didn't get any better. The two of them never stopped squabbling. I got out the eggs and the milk to make pancake batter. Gretel snatched the jug and spilt milk all over the floor. Then she walked in it. Hansel stepped on Wilson's tail and didn't say sorry. They were still too busy fighting about who would be first to toss the pancakes. Gretel kicked Hansel in the shin and he got back at her by breaking an egg on her head. She cried and pinched him on the arm. He pulled her hair.

"Look," I snapped. "If you two don't behave yourselves, there won't be any pancakes."

Gretel folded her arms, pouted, and went into a sulk.

"In that case, I won't be staying," said Hansel and marched to the door. He struggled with the knob, then said, "It won't open. What's going on?"

"I used a locking spell," I told him. "You're my prisoners now. If you look in that corner, you'll see a tall, pointy hat and a broomstick. What does that tell you?"

"You're a witch!" cried Gretel, and burst into tears again. Wilson fled upstairs, where it was quiet.

"Nonsense," said Hansel. "Open this door, vile old woman, or it will be the worst for you."

Now, I don't like being threatened, especially by hoity-toity children. I'm a witch. I deserve respect.

"Less of your back chat, young man," I snapped. "You're not at home now, you know."

"Wait till my parents here about this," he said. "You'll be in trouble."

"Not as much trouble as you're in now," I told him.

Do you know what he did then? He started to kick the door. BANG! BANG! BANG! Between that and Gretel crying, I thought I'd go mad.

I grabbed him by the collar and put my face close to his.

"Hansel," I said. "I am giving you a warning. If you don't stop this now, I will lock you in the naughty shed. I mean it, mind."

He pulled away and attempted another run at the door. I almost caught him, but Gretel grabbed my apron string to hold me back, so the tip of his boot connected. BANG! The wood splintered. Flakes of paint showered down.

That did it. I was wild.

Ten minutes later, Hansel was locked in the shed. There's a little grate set in the door, and his angry red face pressed up against it as I walked away.

"Let me out!" he screamed. "Let me out, you wicked old witch!"

I went back into the house, where Gretel was throwing a tantrum. She lay face down, hammered the floor with her fists and howled.

"Get up," I said, my voice brisk. "Wash your face and hair in the sink. You're covered in egg and chocolate. Hands too. We need clean hands for cooking."

"We're cooking?" said Gretel. She stopped howling and sat up.

"Indeed," I said. "I said we'd make pancakes and that's what we'll do. I'll teach you how make good ones."

And I did. She was a bit slow and clumsy, but she seemed to enjoy herself. She told me that they never cooked at home. She said that they lived on takeaways because both her parents went out to work. Nothing wrong with parents working, of course. But I got the feeling that Hansel and Gretel were thrown into each other's company a lot. And their parents didn't seem to check them much. They had plenty of toys, she told me, but not a lot of time with their mum and dad. They ran way all the time, just for something to do.

The pancakes turned out fine. We ate them with sugar and lemon. Gretel washed up. She was yawning and looking a bit tired, but she wanted to do it herself.

I took a plate of pancakes out to Hansel, who started up with his nonsense again the moment he saw me.

"Brute!" he shouted. "Kidnapper!"

I said, "Do you want these pancakes or shall I take them away?"

He said, "Do they have sugar on?"

I said, "They do. And lemon."

He said, "Do you have any chocolate spread?"

I said, "No." If there's one thing I can't stand, it's a faddy eater.

He said, "All right. I'll have them I suppose."

I said, "What's the magic word?"

He said, "All right. Please."

I passed them through the grate and walked away.

He rattled the bars, kicked at the door and shouted, "How long do I have to stay in here?"

I said, "Until you stop kicking other people's property. You have to learn that bad behaviour has consequences. Goodnight." And I went back indoors.

Gretel and Wilson were playing with a piece of string.

She said, "Is Hansel all right? Did he like the pancakes?" She sounded all sweet and hopeful.

I said, "Yes. He loved them." And she beamed from ear to ear. When she's not crying, she's really not that bad.

She said, "He's not always like that. Only when he gets too tired."

I said, "Indeed. He needs a good night's sleep. We all do."

I made up a bed in the spare room. We each had a glass of warm milk. I read Gretel a story about evil fairies, which she enjoyed. Wilson sat on her lap and followed her upstairs when she went to bed.

I checked on Hansel before I turned in. I wasn't worried about him getting cold. There are plenty of old sacks in the shed.

I listened at the shed door. From the floor, there came the sound of heavy snoring. He was all right, then. He would be a lot less uppity in the morning, after a good night's sleep. I know how *I* feel when I stay up until all hours.

I looked in on Gretel. She was fast asleep too. Wilson was curled up on the bottom of the bed.

Result!

Chapter 5
What Next?

The next morning, Gretel and I had porridge for breakfast, with cream and sugar. She looked much better now her face and hair were clean. She had two bowls of porridge. We followed that with toast and honey. Then we cleared away the plates together. She washed and I dried. Then I showed her how to lay the fire. I let her light it with the matches. She loved that.

I left her showing Wilson the pictures in the evil fairy book and went to check on Hansel.

His face was already at the grate. He wasn't so red now. He looked pale, and a bit worried.

I said, "Morning. Sleep well?"

He said, "When do I get out?"

I said, "We'll see. What do you want for breakfast?"

He said, "What is there?"

I said, "Healthy porridge."

He said, "Is that all?"

I said, "Yes. Take it or leave it, up to you."

He said, "Alright. I suppose so. I mean – um – yes, please."

Hey! We were getting somewhere!

I took him out a bowl of porridge and passed it through the bars. He grabbed at it. I held on.

I said, "What do we say?"

He mumbled, "Thank you."

His manners were a lot better already. I would let him out if he kept it up.

To my surprise, Gretel offered to go around the house peeling off flies. I was pleased about that, as it's not a job I enjoy. While she was gone, I drew up a chart on a big sheet of paper, which I pinned to the wall. I listed all the jobs that needed doing around the house, together with Hansel and Gretel's names. Each time they finished a task, they would get a gold star. If they got ten stars, they would get a treat. Good idea, eh?

Gretel came in with a basket of dead flies, and got a star right away. I explained the chart system to her, and she was thrilled. I left her combing Wilson's tail and went to the wood shed.

"May I come out now, please?" asked Hansel, in a very polite manner. "I'm very sorry."

"Of course," I said. I unlocked the door and he stepped out, looking nervous. I pushed his hat down over his eyes for a joke, and he smiled a bit. I took his hand. "Come on. Cheer up. Let's go in the house and I'll show you this lovely chart I've made."

Like Gretel, he was quite taken with the chart. Both of them stood quietly while I told them again how it worked.

"Right," Hansel said. "I'll go and chop some wood, then. That's a man's job."

Gretel opened her mouth to argue, caught my eye and shut it again.

"Gretel," I said. "I wonder if you would be so kind as to fetch in a bucket of water from the pump? The kettle needs filling. I'm gasping for a cup of tea."

"Of course, Old Maggit," she said, and ran off. I sat down with the newspaper and Wilson on my lap and left them to get on with the chores. It was wonderful.

We had home-made soup, bread, cheese and apples for lunch. We sat nicely at the table and had a very pleasant conversation. We passed each other things and said "please" and "thank you." They told me about their favourite colours and what they wanted for their birthdays. I told them about the Wickedest Witch contest. They were very interested. I told them all about the entry form, and the many years of no luck. I told them a bit about the witches who got through most years. Those were the ones who sneered at me for not even making the short list.

"So you have to do something really, *really* wicked?" asked Gretel, with wide eyes.

"Yep," I said. "The sweet house was just for starters. Now I have to decide what happens next. With you two, I mean. It's a bit of a problem."

"You could send a ransom note," said Hansel. "Our parents will pay up. But I think they might be on holiday. They might not get it for weeks."

I hadn't thought of that.

"You could sell us as slaves," said Gretel. "To a pirate captain. *You'd* like that, wouldn't you, Hansel?" She turned to me and whispered, "He's always wanted to run away to sea."

"I don't know any pirates," I said. "Sorry."

"You could eat us," was Hansel's next idea. "Only joking," he added.

Gretel and I laughed.

I said, "Not likely. That daft feather on your hat might get stuck in my throat. Anyway, all that cheese has quite filled me up."

"Well," said Gretel, "You go and put your feet up, Old Maggit. We'll have a think about it, won't we, Hansel? While we finish the chores."

This was working out even better than I had imagined. Not only were they doing all my work, they were also doing my *thinking* for me.

"Another gold star each!" I cried, and sat down with the crossword puzzle.

Chapter 6
The Plan

By supper time, the house was as clean as a new pin. There was a pile of logs by the back door, loose sweets had been swept up, the garden was free of weeds, the chimney had been swept and Wilson had been brushed to within an inch of his life. Between them, Hansel and Gretel had earned nine stars each. Even better, they hadn't squabbled while they were doing it. They even helped each other out. Gretel sang as she worked. She had a terrible voice, but it was nice to see her happy. Hansel gave her kind little pats on the head whenever he went by. It was quite heart-warming.

We had baked potatoes for supper. I had a feeling crispy spiders wouldn't appeal to children.

"Old Maggit," said Hansel, as he cleared the plates away (without being asked). "We've been thinking about your problem."

"You have?" I said.

"Yes. We think we've come up with the answer."

"Really?"

"Yes. We think you should tell a big, fat lie on the entry form."

"You do?"

"Yes. We think you should say that you locked me in the woodshed and fattened me up."

"And made me be your slave," added Gretel, excited.

"And then say that you heated up the oven ready to cook and eat me," shouted Hansel.

"We know you wouldn't, of course," said Gretel. "Not really. It's only a story."

"So what do you think?" asked Hansel.

"I like it," I said. "It's got drama. It's got horror. It's got cannibalism. I'm pretty sure it's a winner. There's only one thing wrong with it."

"What's that?" they chorused.

"Well – that would be the end of you two, wouldn't it?" I said. "You'd never be able to show your faces again. Not if you'd been cooked and eaten. The second anyone saw you alive and kicking, it would all come out. I wouldn't be the Wickedest Witch in the World. I'd be a laughing stock."

They both thought about this.

"You could say we tricked you in the end," said Hansel. "We could make up a story where – I don't know – something like, Gretel could act stupid and say she didn't know whether the stove was hot yet, and you could look in, and she could push you inside."

"Pushed inside my own oven?" I said. "Hmm. Wouldn't work. You see, that would mean *I'd* be a goner. I'd have trouble filling forms in if I was burnt to a crisp."

"You could say you used a spell to put the fire out," said Gretel. "Then it would be a happy ending for all of us." For a six-year-old, she came up with some good ideas.

"And even if you don't kill us in the end, the wicked *plan* was there," said Hansel. "That's what's important."

"You know, you could be right," I said. "It might just work. As long as the pair of you promise never to breathe a word of it to anyone."

"Of course we won't!" said Gretel, shocked. "It will be our secret."

"I'll help you fill in the entry form, if you like," offered Hansel. "I've got very neat writing."

"Excellent!" I cried. "Another gold star for each of you! That means you get a treat. What would you like?"

They opted for a go on my broomstick. Fair enough. We all squeezed on and had a nice little ride over the forest by the light of the moon. They giggled and screamed and we did a loop the loop, which I haven't tried in years. Hansel lost his hat. Gretel shouted, "Again! Do it again!"

It was a right laugh. A bit chilly, though.

Chapter 7
How It Ended

They went home the next day. Hansel promised to post my entry form when they passed a post box. I offered them a basket full of sweets off the house, but they said no, thank you. I couldn't blame them. It was a warm day and the chocolate tiles were beginning to melt. Brown streaks oozed down the walls. Squirrels had been at the marzipan. The birds had picked off *all* the Smarties, not just the red ones. The house was definitely past its best.

"We'd like a slice of your home-made bread and a flask of soup, though," said Hansel. "If it's not too much trouble."

"Of course," I said. "It will be a pleasure." Well, I do make good soup.

Gretel gave me a big hug and said she wished I was her Nan. Hansel showed me how to do something called a 'high five'. Gretel asked if she could come and visit Wilson. I told her she could, but it had to be a secret. Hansel wanted to come and chop more logs in a couple of days. I told them both to leave it until I had a reply from the people at the Wickedest Witch contest. I didn't want to get put out at the last minute. You're not supposed to get visits from your victims.

We parted at the garden gate. They ran off hand-in-hand. I stood there waving, long after they vanished into the trees. Then I went in and took down the chart, put away the jar of gold stars and made myself a cup of tea.

I have to say, Wilson and I felt a bit lonely.

The next day, Frank, Ted and Rocky came to strip all the soggy gingerbread and the last mucky sweets off the house. Once that was done, there was nothing left to do. Everything went back to normal. No one called. I would have been glad of some company.

I cheered up when the postman arrived a week or so later with my invite to enter the contest. At long last, I was a contender! The big cheeses had believed the story we had concocted! They sounded rather impressed. I was in with an excellent chance.

Well, you know what happened. I showed up, and I won!

So. Here I am, gazing at my silver cup and wondering what to do with a rubber worm, some sparklers and set of plastic fingernails. Wilson's popped the balloon already.

Hang on! What's that? I think I heard the gate squeak! Could it be ...?

"Old Maggit!" comes Gretel's voice. "It's us! Did you win? Oh, do say you won!"

"Ready for some more logs?" shouts Hansel. "I've brought a better axe!"

Wilson leaps off my lap with a happy mew and runs to the door.

Yes. I'm the Wickedest Witch in the World – but children love me.

How weird is that?

Our books are tested
for children and young people by
children and young people.

Thanks to everyone who consulted on
a manuscript for their time and effort in
helping us to make our books better
for our readers.

More from **Kaye Umansky**...

The Queen's Tale

Three things Snow White's new stepmother is a fan of: 1. shopping, 2. clothes, 3. being the Fairest in the Land.

Three things Snow White's new stepmother is NOT a fan of: 1. Snow White, 2. Snow White, 3. Snow White.

Skin as white as snow, hair as black as ebony and lips as red as blood? How very last season. Snow White has got to go.

It's Poison Apple Time!

This is *Snow White* as you've never read it before.

The Stepsisters' Story

Move over Cinders –
the Stepsisters are here!

Lardine and Angula have their sights set on the Prince. No stupid servant's going to stand in their way...

This is *Cinderella*
as you've never read it before.

www.barringtonstoke.co.uk